COYOTE in LOVE
with a STAR

Story by Marty Kreipe de Montaño
Illustrations by Tom Coffin

Tales of the People

National Museum of the American Indian,
Smithsonian Institution
Washington, D.C., and New York

Abbeville Press   Publishers
New York   London   Paris

Ol' Man Coyote was coming along, they say, following the dusty road next to the pasture. He was hungry, as usual. Unemployment was high on the Potawatomi reservation, and he couldn't find a job. A friend of his who had been to New York City told him there were lots of jobs there. They even paid people to open doors and run elevators. He figured that with his skills he could easily get a job.

Coyote was also a little lonely and hoped maybe he could find someone special in the big city.

He cooked up a big batch of fry bread and stuffed it into a brown paper bag. He loaded his cast-iron skillet, his bag of fry bread, and his Pendleton blanket into his VW van. Then he took off down the bumpy lane, past the barn and the horse pasture, crossed Little Soldier Creek, and headed toward the place where the sun comes up.

Coyote drove and drove, camping along the way, eating fry bread, and sleeping in his blanket. The farther from Kansas he traveled, the wider the road became, until it was a huge highway stretching to the horizon.

The closer he got to New York City, the faster the cars went. Everyone seemed to be speeding along. With his heart pounding, Coyote drove over the George Washington Bridge and entered a different world.

Tall buildings blocked the sun. Loud music boomed from every corner. The sidewalks were full of people, and they were all in a big hurry. There were many neighborhoods, each one like a different country, with its own food, smells, language, and music.

After Coyote found a place to stay and got himself settled, he took to the streets, looking for work. Walking along Broadway, he came to a set of stairs that went down into the ground. As he peered into this deep hole, he could hear a rumbling and he felt the ground tremble. Something big was down there, for sure. It sounded like a whole herd of buffalo.

He climbed down the steps. At the bottom Coyote saw a tall fence with iron bars, and beyond that was a long silver train with lots of people pushing their way on and off.

15

Tired and footsore, he wanted to ride that train. He saw some men pushing grocery carts full of flowers through a gate in the fence. Coyote the trickster had an idea—he would change himself into a sunflower! He did and, sure enough, one of the flower sellers picked him up and put him in his basket. Safe among the flowers, Coyote boarded the train.

When the train reached the last stop, everyone rushed out the
doors. Coyote changed back into himself and followed the crowd.
Soon he was staring up at two huge towers that stretched to the
sky. The lobby of the tower was packed with people going to
work. Surely someone with all his skills could get hired too.

Coyote was right. He found a job, and it was in his field, too. He became the Rodent Control Officer in the World Trade Center.

But he was always homesick. On clear nights, Coyote would escape the noise and hurry of the city by going up to the observation deck to watch the stars as they danced across the sky.

Once, when the stars came very close, he noticed one star that was more beautiful than all the rest. She was so beautiful that Coyote fell in love with her.

Every night when the stars came out, Coyote waited until the beautiful star came near the observation deck, and then he howled and howled, begging her to take him up into the sky. He wanted to dance with her.

At first she just ignored him. But one night, after he pleaded and begged, the star danced over and pulled him into the sky, and they began to dance together.

As they danced across the sky, he was so happy he thought his heart would burst.

After a while, Coyote began to realize that the star wouldn't talk to him. The stars didn't even talk to each other—they just danced, cold and beautiful, across the night sky.

Then he noticed how cold it was, and when he looked down, he got dizzy. Shivering and scared, he just wanted to return to earth. He begged the star to let him go home. At last she danced with him over to the edge of the sky. And then the star dropped him.

Coyote fell down and down, for four days and four nights.

Coyote kept falling, and when he got closer to the earth, he saw that he was heading straight for Central Park. When his body hit the ground, it made a great big hole. And when that hole filled with water, it became known as the Reservoir.

And that's what became of Ol' Man Coyote.

So now, whenever you hear coyotes howling at the night sky, you know they're scolding the star that dropped their grandfather.

That's what the people say.

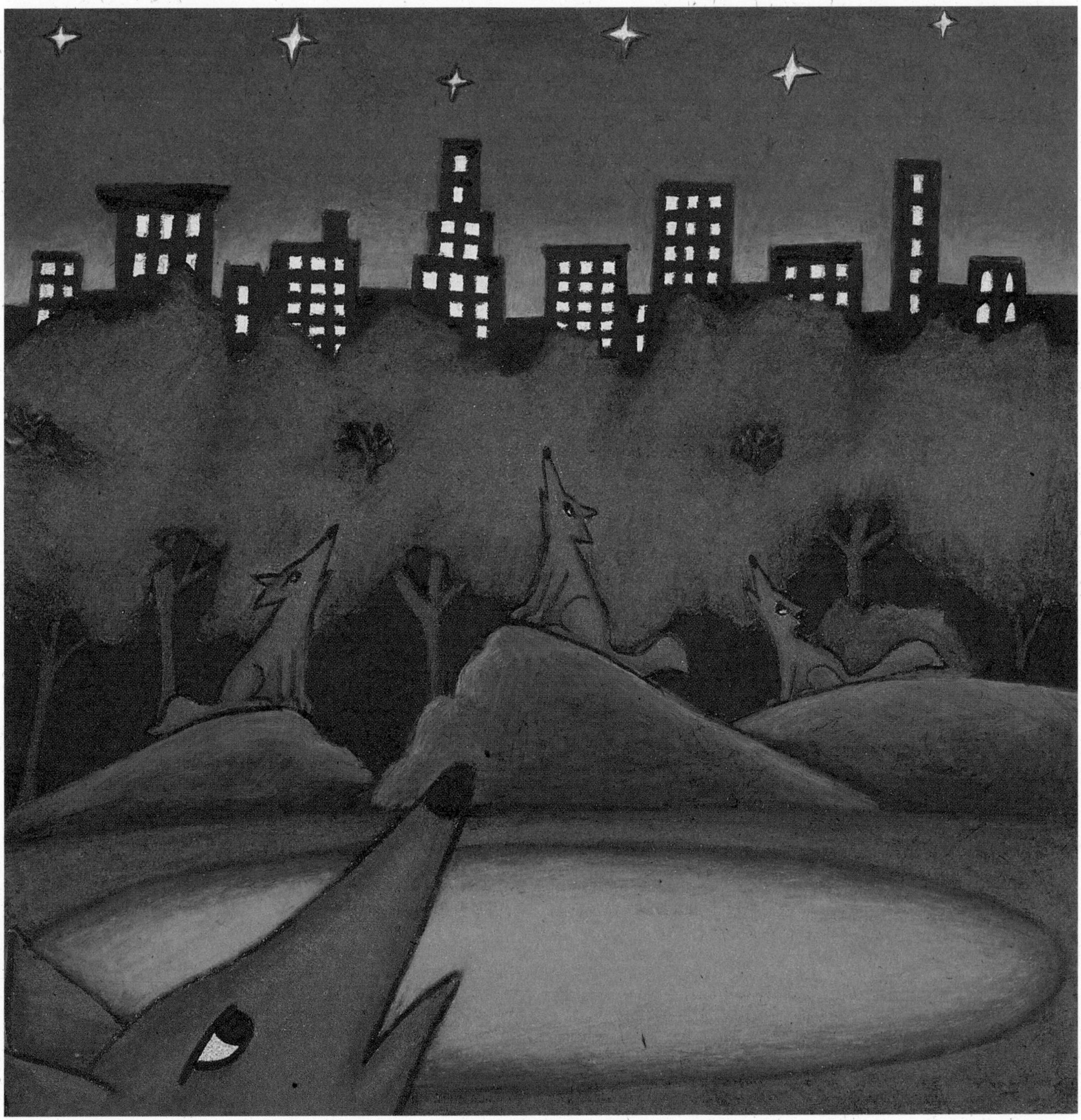

Coyote the Trickster

Long ago, before we had television and books, before anybody wrote our languages down, everything was learned by listening and doing. The spoken word was very important, and listening to stories was like going to school, to the movies, and to church, all at the same time.

Then, as now, stories would talk about things like how the world was created and what our role in the world is. Indian ideas of what is considered proper behavior are reinforced by stories that poke fun at foolish misbehavior. Indian people use many kinds of stories to tell their histories, and in many ways their stories are America's only truly native literature.

Haida dance rattle, c. 1850–75. Skidegate, Queen Charlotte Island, British Columbia, Canada. Carved cedar wood fiber, length: 12³/₄ in. (32.5 cm). 1.8028.

A trickster-hero's exploits figure in the tales told by many tribal nations in North America. The American Indian trickster-hero may be responsible for creating parts of the world, but at the same time he often misbehaves. Different people give him different identities. He is Spider to the Sioux, he is Raven on the Northwest Coast. The people of the Great Lakes call him Hare, and to many people in the West he is Coyote.

The Coyote story told here is an adaptation of a traditional tale that is told in various ways. One version is from the Klamath of southern Oregon, who use it to explain the creation of Crater Lake. I have brought the story into the present and have made it somewhat autobiographical.

Kwagu'ł (Kwakiutl) mask representing Raven, late 19th/ early 20th century. Vancouver Island, British Columbia, Canada. Length: 35 in. (89 cm). 1.2180.

—Marty Kreipe de Montaño

Glossary

The trickster-hero has different names in different languages:

Blackfoot	*Napi*
Cree	*Wisah Kicáh*
Delaware	*Wehixamukes*
Eastern Cree	*Wee-sa-key-jac*
Innu	*Kwakwadjec*
Kiowa	*Sanaday*
Mi'kmaq	*Gluskap*
Nez Perce	*ʔiceyé.ye*
Potawatomi	*Nanabush*
Salish	*Smiyáw*
Sioux	*Iktomi*
Spokane	*Spílye*
Yuma-Quechan	*Xatalwé*
Zuni	*Suski*

O-o-be (Kiowa), 1895. Fort Sill, Oklahoma. P13149.

Many Plains tribes decorated girls' and women's dresses with elk teeth. Each elk had only two of the type of teeth used for adornment, and this scarcity made the teeth—and the garments they decorated—very valuable.

Blackfoot boys, c. 1910. N21900.

Most of the boys in this photograph are wearing at least some traditional garments, although each boy's attire also shows Western influences. The boy on the left—with his Western-style clothes and haircut—was probably a student at an Indian boarding school.

The Potawatomi

The name of the Potawatomi tribe is a version of the Ojibwe word *potawatomink,* meaning "People of the Place of Fire." That name comes from the Potawatomis' role as keepers of the council fire in their early alliance with the closely related Ottawa and Ojibwe tribes. In their own language, the Potawatomi call themselves *Nishnabek,* or "People." Today there are seven bands of Potawatomi—one in Canada and six in the United States—with a total of about 24,200 members. Originally Algonquin speakers who lived in the Great Lakes region, the Potawatomi were among the many tribes forced by the pressure of white settlements to move west of the Mississippi in the 1830s. Some Potawatomi groups fled to Canada; many others were moved to reservations in Oklahoma and Kansas.

In traditional Potawatomi society, the people provided for themselves with game, fish, wild rice, red oak acorns, and maple syrup. Potawatomi women learned to cultivate corn, beans, and squash, and they were known for their medicinal herb gardens.

In summer the Potawatomi lived in villages of rectangular houses covered with bark or woven brush. After a buffalo hunt in the fall, they would divide into small hunting camps and live during the winter in oval, dome-shaped wigwams.

Potawatomi beaded bandolier bag. 45 x 14¼ in. (113.8 x 35.9 cm). 14.2144.

It can take an entire year or more to make a heavily beaded bandolier bag like this one. Making a bag is often a family project or may be shared between mother and daughter.

Above: *Prairie Potawatomi doll, late 19th/early 20th century. Kansas. Hide, horsehair, cloth, silk ribbon, beads, animal claw, German-silver ornaments, wood, and vermilion, height: 10¼ in. (25.8 cm).* 24.1799.

Right: *Potawatomi wigwam with bark and reed covering, Wabeno, Wisconsin.* P22003.

Housing design, shaped by cultural beliefs as well as by geography and climate, was a primary form of expression among Native American cultures. This dwelling is the type of house built by the Potawatomi in the Great Lakes region.